Pretty little Girls

All Over the World!

AuthorHouse™
1663 Liberty Drive
Bloomington, IN 47403
www.authorhouse.com
Phone: 833-262-8899

Because of the dynamic nature of the Internet, any web addresses or links contained in
this book may have changed since publication and may no longer be valid. The views
expressed in this work are solely those of the author and do not necessarily reflect the
views of the publisher, and the publisher hereby disclaims any responsibility for them.

Any people depicted in stock imagery provided by Getty Images are models,
and such images are being used for illustrative purposes only.
Certain stock imagery © Getty Images.

This book is printed on acid-free paper.

ISBN: 979-8-8230-2572-0 (sc)

Print information available on the last page.

Published by AuthorHouse 06/14/2024

authorHOUSE®

Pretty Little Girls

All Over The World

Written by Olivia Lee

Illustrated by Natalia Wellman

Pretty little girls, come and see!

They look like you!

They look like me!

Come on, follow me!

Around the world we'll go!

First let's stop and have some tea!

Such pretty little girls with...

braids, pigtails, blonde curls,

and ponytails!

Brown hair, red hair, we are everywhere!

Look! There's the fair!

Look we're at the park!

At the beach!

Ohh! Yippie! Ice cream treats!

Let's ride bikes

and fly kites!

We love Kittens!

Wait put on your mittens!!

There's a princess!

I love your pretty dress!

Ooh, a rockstar with a guitar!

She's driving a car!

Oh my, what are we to do?

I see a ballerina too!!

Pretty little girls love skates!

We help Mom bake cakes!

And we ride bikes! Yikes!!

Here we are in frills and lace,

And lip gloss with

bubble gum taste!

We're glitz and glam,
and like to play dress-up,
diamonds and pearls
and hair like candy-cane swirls!

Off to an adventure!

Let's go fish with Dad!

Ugh! Worms!

Ugh! Germs!

So many things to do!!

Gotta learn to tie my shoe!

Hurry!! We're going to the pool to swim!

Wait! I'm going to climb that tree

and swing from the limb!

We can be friends, you and me!

We are pretty little girls all over the world!

And even though we're different, we are all the same in so many ways!

How?

In what ways?

Well here's a surprise!

What do you think?

Now Open!

Dedicated to my beautiful granddaughters:

India, Iyana and Iniya

I love you with the core of my being.

Be good-do good.

O. Lee

Olivia Lee is a grandmother of three wonderful girls residing in Florida. She retired from the telecommunications industry after 38 years and decided to pursue her love of writing which for her was a "gift from God" spanning back some 48 years ago. As a teenager she first discovered the joy of words and writing. A personal endeavor, she hopes to capture the innocent hearts and minds of young readers all over the world, showing them the many qualities they all share.

Printed in the United States
by Baker & Taylor Publisher Services